CATHERINE STORR was born in 1913. She was educated at St Paul's Girls' School in London and then at Newnham College, Cambridge, where she read English Literature. Although her ambition was always to be a writer, she decided to study medicine and went on to work as a psychotherapist. Catherine was married in 1942 and in the same year had the first of her three daughters. She returned to her writing and created short stories for her young daughters, including the adventures of *Clever Polly and the Stupid Wolf*, which has remained in print ever since it was first published in 1955. Catherine wrote more than thirty much-loved books for children and young adults, which have been translated into many different languages. She died in 2001, aged eighty-seven.

Books by Catherine Storr

CLEVER POLLY AND THE STUPID WOLF
POLLY AND THE WOLF AGAIN

CATHERINE STORR

CLEVER POLLY AND THE STUPID WOLF

Illustrated by Marjorie-Ann Watts

A PUFFIN BOOK

PUFFIN BOOKS

UK | USA | Canada | Ireland | Australia
India | New Zealand | South Africa

Puffin Books is part of the Penguin Random House group of companies
whose addresses can be found at global.penguinrandomhouse.com.

puffinbooks.com

First published by Faber and Faber 1955
Published in Puffin Books 1967
Reissued in this edition 2015

002

Set in 13.5/20.5 pt Sabon LT Std
Typeset by Jouve (UK), Milton Keynes
Printed in Great Britain by Clays Ltd, St Ives plc

A CIP catalogue record for this book is available from the British Library

ISBN: 978-0-141-36023-2

www.greenpenguin.co.uk

Penguin Random House is committed to a
sustainable future for our business, our readers
and our planet. This book is made from Forest
Stewardship Council® certified paper.

Contents

1. The First Story

THIS book has twelve stories about Polly and how she always managed to escape from the wolf by being cleverer than he was – which wasn't very difficult because he was generally not at all clever. In fact he was rather stupid.

The very first story of all, which tells about how Polly met the wolf for the first time, has really been told already, in a book called *Clever Polly*. But because it's very annoying not to know how things started and how the people you are reading about met each other in the beginning, I'm going to put it in here. So really this book has thirteen stories about Polly and the wolf and that is all the stories there are at present about them.

This first story is a very small story because Polly was very small when it happened, so the story was just big enough to match her. And here it is.

2. Clever Polly

ONE DAY Polly was alone downstairs. Camilla was using the Hoover upstairs, so when the front doorbell rang, Polly went to open the door. There was a great black wolf! He put his foot inside the door and said:

'Now I'm going to eat you up!'

'Oh no, please,' said Polly. 'I don't want to be eaten up.'

'Oh, yes,' said the wolf, 'I am going to eat you. But first tell me, what is that delicious smell?'

'Come down to the kitchen,' said Polly, 'and I will show you.'

She led the wolf down to the kitchen. There on the table was a delicious-looking pie.

'Have a slice?' said Polly. The wolf's mouth watered, and he said, 'Yes, please!' Polly cut him a big piece. When he had eaten it, the wolf asked for another, and then for another.

'Now,' said Polly, after the third helping, 'what about me?'

'Sorry,' said the wolf, 'I'm too full of pie. I'll come back another day to deal with you.'

A week later Polly was alone again, and again the bell rang. Polly ran to open the door. There was the wolf again.

'This time I'm really going to eat you up, Polly,' said the wolf.

'All right,' said Polly, 'but first, just smell.'

The wolf took a long breath. 'Delicious!' he said. 'What is it?'

'Come down and see,' said Polly.

In the kitchen was a large chocolate cake.

'Have a slice?' said Polly.

'Yes,' said the wolf greedily. He ate six big slices.

'Now, what about me?' said Polly.

'Sorry,' said the wolf, 'I just haven't got room. I'll come back.' He slunk out of the back door.

A week later the doorbell rang again. Polly opened the door, and there was the wolf.

'Now this time you shan't escape me!' he snarled. 'Get ready to be eaten up now!'

'Just smell all round first,' said Polly gently.

'Marvellous!' admitted the wolf. 'What is it?'

'Toffee,' said Polly calmly. 'But come on, eat me up.'

'Couldn't I have a tiny bit of toffee first?' asked the wolf. 'It's my favourite food.'

'Come down and see,' said Polly.

The wolf followed her downstairs. The toffee bubbled and sizzled on the stove. 'I must have a taste,' said the wolf.

'It's hot,' said Polly.

The wolf took the spoon out of the saucepan and put it in his mouth:

OW! HOWL! OW!

It was so hot it burnt the skin off his mouth and tongue and he couldn't spit it out, it was too sticky. In terror, the wolf ran out of the house and NEVER CAME BACK!

3. Clever Polly and the Stupid Wolf

D ID I say that the wolf never came back? I'm wrong, he did come back a year or two later. This time Polly was sitting at the window of the drawing-room and she saw the wolf open the garden gate and glance anxiously around. He looked up and saw Polly.

'Good morning, Polly,' said the wolf.

'Good morning, Wolf,' said Polly. 'What have you come here for?'

'I have come to eat you up,' replied the wolf. 'And this time I'm going to get you.'

Polly smiled. She knew that last time she had been cleverer than the wolf and she was not really frightened.

'I'm not going to eat you up this morning,' said the wolf. 'I'm going to come back in the middle of the night and climb in at your bedroom window and gobble you up. By the way,' said the wolf, 'which is your bedroom window?'

'That one,' said Polly, pointing upwards. 'Right at the top of the house. You'll find it rather difficult, won't you, to get right up there?'

Then the wolf smiled. 'I'm cleverer than you think,' he said. 'I thought it would probably mean climbing and I have come prepared.'

Polly saw him go to a flower bed and make a little hole in the earth. Into the hole he dropped something, she couldn't see what, and covered it carefully up again.

'Wolf,' said Polly, 'what were you doing then?'

'Oh,' said the wolf, 'this is my great cleverness. I have planted a pip of a grape. This pip will grow into a vine and the vine will climb up the house and I shall climb up the vine. I shall pop in through your bedroom window and then, Polly, I shall get you at last.'

Polly laughed. 'Poor Wolf,' she said. 'Do you know how long it will take for that pip to grow into a vine?'

'No,' said the wolf. 'Two or three days? I'm very hungry.'

'Perhaps,' said Polly, 'in a week or two a little shoot might poke its way above the ground, but it would be months before the vine could start climbing and years and years before it could reach my bedroom window.'

'Oh bother!' said the wolf. 'I can't wait years and years and years to reach your bedroom window. I shall have to have another idea even better than this one. Goodbye, Polly, for the present,' and he trotted off.

About a week later Polly was sitting at the drawing-room window again. She was sewing and did not notice the wolf come into the garden until she heard a sort of scrambling noise outside. Then she looked out of the window and saw the wolf very busy planting something in the earth again.

'Good morning, Wolf,' said Polly. 'What are you planting this time?'

'This time,' said the wolf, 'I've had a really good idea. I'm planting something which will grow up to your window in a moment.'

'Oh,' said Polly, interested. 'What is that?'

'I have planted the rung of a ladder,' said the wolf. 'By tomorrow morning there'll be a long ladder stretching right up to your bedroom window. I specially chose a rung from the longest ladder I could see. A steeplejack was on the other end of it climbing a church steeple. He will be surprised when he comes down and finds the bottom rung of his ladder has gone. But in a very short time I shall be climbing in at your bedroom window, little Polly, and that will be the end of *you*.'

Polly laughed. 'Oh, poor Wolf, didn't you know that ladders don't grow from rungs or from anything else? They have to be made by men, and however many rungs you plant in this garden, even of steeplejacks' ladders, they won't grow into anything you could climb up. Go away, Wolf, and have a better idea, if you can.'

The wolf looked very sad. He tucked his tail between his legs and trotted off along the road.

A week later Polly, who now knew what to expect, was sitting at the drawing-room window looking up and down the road.

'What are you waiting for?' asked her mother.

'I'm waiting for that stupid wolf,' said Polly. 'He's sure to come today. I wonder what silly idea he'll have got into his black head now?'

Presently the gate squeaked and the wolf came in carrying something very carefully in his mouth. He put it down on the grass and started to dig a deep hole.

Polly watched him drop the thing he had been carrying into the hole, cover it over with earth again, and stand back with a pleased expression.

'Wolf,' called Polly, 'what have you planted this time?'

'This time,' replied the wolf, 'you aren't going to escape. Have you read "Jack and the Beanstalk", Polly?'

'Well, I haven't exactly read it,' said Polly, 'but I know the story very well indeed.'

'This time,' said the wolf, 'I've planted a bean. Now we know from the story of Jack that beans grow up to the sky in no time at all, and perhaps I shall be in your bedroom before it's light tomorrow morning, crunching up the last of your little bones.'

'A bean!' said Polly, very much interested. 'Where did it come from?'

'I shelled it out of its pod,' said the wolf proudly.

'And the pod?' Polly asked. 'Where did that come from?'

'I bought it in the vegetable shop,' said the wolf, 'with my own money,' he added. 'I bought half a pound, and it cost me a whole sixpence, but I shan't have wasted it because it will bring me a nice, juicy little girl to eat.'

'You bought it?' said Polly. 'Yourself, with your own money?'

'All by myself,' said the wolf grandly.

'No one gave it to you?' Polly insisted.

'No one,' said the wolf. He looked very proud.

'You didn't exchange it for anything?' Polly asked again.

'No,' said the wolf. He was puzzled.

'Oh, poor Wolf,' said Polly pityingly. 'You haven't read "Jack and the Beanstalk" at all. Don't you know that it's only a *magic* bean that grows up to the sky in a night, and you can't buy magic beans. You have to be given them by an old man in exchange for a cow or something like that. It's no good *buying* beans, that won't get you anywhere.'

Two large tears dropped from the wolf's eyes.

'But I haven't *got* a cow,' he cried.

'If you had you wouldn't need to eat me,' Polly pointed out. 'You could eat the cow. It's no good, Wolf, you aren't going to get me this time. Come back in a month or two, and we'll have a bean-feast off the plant you've just planted.'

'I hate beans,' the wolf sighed, 'and I've got nearly a whole half-pound of them at home.' He turned to go. 'But don't be too cock-a-hoop, Miss Polly, for I'll get you yet!'

But clever Polly knew he never would.

4. Little Polly Riding Hood

ONCE every two weeks Polly went over to the other side of the town to see her grandmother. Sometimes she took a small present, and sometimes she came back with a small present for herself. Sometimes all the rest of the family went too, and sometimes Polly went alone.

One day, when she was going by herself, she had hardly got down the front doorsteps when she saw the wolf.

'Good afternoon, Polly,' said the wolf. 'Where are you going to, may I ask?'

'Certainly,' said Polly. 'I'm going to see my grandma.'

'I thought so!' said the wolf, looking very much pleased. 'I've been reading about a little girl who went to visit her grandmother and it's a very good story.'

'Little Red Riding Hood?' suggested Polly.

'That's it!' cried the wolf. 'I read it out loud to myself as a bedtime story. I did enjoy it. The wolf eats up the grandmother *and* Little Red Riding Hood. It's almost the only story where a wolf really gets anything to eat,' he added sadly.

'But in my book he doesn't get Red Riding Hood,' said Polly. 'Her father comes in just in time to save her.'

'Oh, he doesn't in *my* book!' said the wolf. 'I expect mine is the true story, and yours is just invented. Anyway, it seems a good idea.'

'What is a good idea?' asked Polly.

'To catch little girls on their way to their grandmothers' cottages,' said the wolf. 'Now where had I got to?'

'I don't know what you mean,' said Polly.

'Well, I'd said, "Where are you going to?",' said the wolf. 'Oh yes. Now I must say, "Where does she live?". Where does your grandmother live, Polly Riding Hood?'

'Over the other side of the town,' answered Polly.

The wolf frowned.

'It ought to be "Through the wood",' he said. 'But perhaps town will do. How do you get there, Polly Riding Hood?'

'First I take a train and then I take a bus,' said Polly.

The wolf stamped his foot.

'No, no, no, no!' he shouted. 'That's all wrong. You can't say that. You've got to say, "By that path winding through the trees", or something like that. You can't go by trains and buses and things. It isn't fair.'

'Well, I could say that,' said Polly, 'but it wouldn't be true. I do have to go by bus and train to see my grandma, so what's the good of saying I don't?'

'But then it won't work,' said the wolf impatiently. 'How can I get there first and gobble her up and get all dressed up to trick you into believing I am her if we've got a great train journey to do? And anyhow I haven't any money on me, so I can't even take a ticket. You just can't say that.'

'All right, I won't say it,' said Polly agreeably. 'But it's true all the same. Now just excuse me, Wolf, I've got to get down to the station because I am going to visit my grandma even if you aren't.'

The wolf slunk along behind Polly, growling to himself. He stood just behind her at the booking-office and heard her ask for her ticket, but he could not go any further. Polly got into a train and was carried away, and the wolf went sadly home.

But just two weeks later the wolf was waiting outside Polly's house again. This time he had plenty of change in his pocket. He even had a book tucked under his front leg to read in the train.

He partly hid himself behind a corner of brick wall and watched to see Polly come out on her way to her grandmother's house.

But Polly did not come out alone, as she had before. This time the whole family appeared, Polly's father and mother too. They got into the car, which was waiting in the road, and Polly's father started the engine.

The wolf ran along behind his brick wall as fast as he could, and was just in time to get out into the road ahead of the car, and to stand waving his paws as if he wanted a lift as the car came up.

Polly's father slowed down, and Polly's mother put her head out of the window.

'Where do you want to go?' she asked.

'I want to go to Polly's grandmother's house,' the wolf answered. His eyes glistened as he looked at the family of plump little girls in the back of the car.

'That's where we are going,' said her mother, surprised. 'Do you know her then?'

'Oh no,' said the wolf. 'But you see, I want to get there very quickly and eat her up and then I can put on her clothes and wait for Polly, and eat her up too.'

'Good heavens!' said Polly's father. 'What a horrible idea! We certainly shan't give you a lift if that is what you are planning to do.'

Polly's mother screwed up the window again and Polly's father drove quickly on. The wolf was left standing miserably in the road.

'Bother!' he said to himself angrily. 'It's gone wrong again. I can't think why it can't be the same as the Little Red Riding Hood story. It's all these buses and cars and trains that make it go wrong.'

But the wolf was determined to get Polly, and when she was due to visit her grandmother again, a fortnight later, he went down and took a ticket for the station he had heard Polly ask for. When he got out of the train, he climbed on a bus, and soon he was walking down the road where Polly's grandmother lived.

'Aha!' he said to himself, 'this time I shall get them both. First the grandma, then Polly.'

He unlatched the gate into the garden, and strolled up the path to Polly's grandmother's front door. He rapped sharply with the knocker.

'Who's there?' called a voice from inside the house.

The wolf was very much pleased. This was going just as it had in the story. This time there would be no mistakes.

'Little Polly Riding Hood,' he said in a squeaky voice. 'Come to see her dear grandmother, with a little present of butter and eggs and – er – cake!'

There was a long pause. Then the voice said doubtfully, '*Who* did you say it was?'

'Little Polly Riding Hood,' said the wolf in a great hurry, quite forgetting to disguise his voice this time. 'Come to eat up her dear grandmother with butter and eggs!'

There was an even longer pause. Then Polly's grandmother put her head out of a window and looked down at the wolf.

'I beg your pardon?' she said.

'I am Polly,' said the wolf firmly.

'Oh,' said Polly's grandma. She appeared to be thinking hard. 'Good afternoon, Polly. Do you know if anyone else happens to

be coming to see me today? A wolf, for instance?'

'No. Yes,' said the wolf in great confusion. 'I met a Polly as I was coming here – I mean, I, Polly, met a wolf on my way here, but she can't have got here yet because I started specially early.'

'That's very queer,' said the grandma. 'Are you quite sure you are Polly?'

'Quite sure,' said the wolf.

'Well, then, I don't know who it is who is here already,' said Polly's grandma. 'She said she was Polly. But if you are Polly then I think this other person must be a wolf.'

'No, no, I am Polly,' said the wolf. 'And, anyhow, you ought not to say all that. You ought to say, "Lift the latch and come in".'

'I don't think I'll do that,' said Polly's grandma. 'Because I don't want my nice little Polly eaten up by a wolf, and if you come in now the wolf who is here already might eat you up.'

Another head looked out of another window. It was Polly's.

'Bad luck, Wolf,' she said. 'You didn't know that I was coming to lunch and tea today instead of just tea as I generally do – so I got here first. And as you are Polly, as you've just said, I must be the wolf, and you'd better run away quickly before I gobble you up, hadn't you?'

'Bother, bother, bother and *bother*!' said the wolf. 'It hasn't worked out right this time either. And I did just what it said in the book. Why can't I ever get you, Polly, when that other wolf managed to get his little girl?'

'Because this isn't a fairy story,' said Polly, 'and I'm not Little Red Riding Hood. I am Polly and I can always escape from you, Wolf, however much you try to catch me.'

'Clever Polly,' said Polly's grandma. And the wolf went growling away.

5. The Visible Wolf

POLLY was walking down the High Street one morning, when on the opposite side of the road she saw the wolf behaving in a very peculiar manner. Sometimes he put out his tongue at passers-by, sometimes he did a few dance steps in the gutter. Several times he seemed to be aiming a blow at someone's head. A few people were turning round to stare at him, but on the whole most of them were too polite to appear to take any notice.

Polly was not afraid of the wolf when there were plenty of other people about, so she

crossed the road and came up to where he
was standing, making faces at a baby in a
perambulator.

'Wolf,' she said, 'you're behaving disgracefully.
What on earth do you think you're doing?'

The wolf jumped about four inches in the
air as Polly spoke and even after he had come
down to earth again he couldn't stop shaking.

'You frightened me,' he said plaintively, his
teeth chattering so that Polly could hear them.
'I didn't expect you to speak to me. How do
you know I am here?'

'Don't be silly,' Polly said impatiently. 'Of course I know you're here. I can see you, for one thing.'

'You can *see* me?' the wolf said, apparently very much surprised.

'Of course I can. And from what I can see you are behaving very badly. I've never seen such an exhibition.'

'But you can't see me,' the wolf protested.

'I certainly can.'

'But I'm invisible.'

Polly was, in her turn, so much surprised that she couldn't speak for a moment. When she could, she asked, 'You're *what*?'

'I'm invisible. You can't see me. No one can!'

'Tell me, Wolf,' Polly asked kindly, 'do you feel quite well? Have you got a headache? The sun has been rather hot this morning.'

'It's not the sun. I'm invisible, I tell you. I don't know how you come to be able to see me, if you really can, but I'm invisible to everyone else.'

'How do you know?' Polly asked.

'Well for one thing, she told me I would be.'

'Who did?'

'The witch I bought the spell from, of course. It was very expensive, but I thought it would be worthwhile. Because now I'm invisible I can come when you aren't suspecting anything and catch you and eat you without any of this arguing. It's always argue argue with you,' the wolf went on sadly. 'As soon as I've got it all nice and clear in my head about when I'm going to eat you, you have to start talking and then I get muddled. Somehow you always seem to get me so that I don't know if I'm coming or going, if I'm full or I'm empty. And it always ends the same way,' he finished disconsolately. 'And that's with you going off scot free and me going off still hungry.'

'So you went to a witch and she made you invisible,' Polly prompted him. 'She can't be much good at her job,' she added.

'She didn't make me invisible there and then. She told me what to do to get invisible.'

'What?'

'Well, I had to go out when the moon was full – that was the day before yesterday – and pick birch bark and mix it with – here!' said the wolf suddenly. 'I'm not going to tell you this spell for nothing. I had to pay for it and if you want it you'll have to pay too.'

'I don't want it,' said Polly. 'Thank you. It obviously isn't any good.'

'Who said so?' said the wolf indignantly.

'I do. It's supposed to make you invisible, isn't it? Well, you're as visible as anything. Anyone can see you. You're as thick and as black and as solid as ever you were.'

'I'm not,' cried the wolf. 'I know I'm not. I've been doing all sorts of things to test it out and I'm sure I'm invisible. No one has taken any notice of me at all; and they would have if they'd seen me.'

'What have you done? I saw you sticking your tongue out and dancing and making silly faces, but what else have you done?'

'You know how I always walk on my hind legs when I'm with people so as to look like them?' the wolf began. 'Well, I walked all the way up from the butcher's to here on four legs and no one so much as turned to look at me.'

'There's no reason why they should,' Polly said. 'They probably thought you were an outsize dog.'

The wolf snorted angrily but he went on:

'I made a horrible face at a baby in a pram and it didn't take any notice at all.'

'I saw you doing that,' Polly agreed. 'If I'd been the baby I'd have made some horrible faces back. But babies get so used to people making faces at them, they don't even look any longer. Go on.'

'You see that drinking-trough for horses over there? I got into that and had a bath with

a piece of soap I happened to have on me. I washed all over, right in front of everyone, and no one blinked an eyelid.'

'They probably agreed that you needed that bath, and in that case they'd be too polite to stare. Is that all you did, Wolf?'

The wolf looked rather sheepish.

'It did seem as if I must be invisible by then,' he said. 'And I wanted to do something people couldn't help being surprised by if they could see it.' He stopped.

'What did you do?' Polly asked encouragingly.

'Of course I know it's childish,' the wolf said. 'It's not a thing I do in the ordinary way.'

'No?'

'Well, I haven't for years. It was just a test, you understand?'

'I expect I will when you tell me what it was.'

'I wanted to be quite out of the ordinary.'

'I daresay it was all most peculiar. But do let me into the secret.'

'I just ran up and down the street a little.'

'Is that all?' Polly asked, disappointed.

'Well, I believe I said "All change", once or twice.'

'All change what?'

'And I had a whistle. Occasionally I used it.'

'I see. You ran, you whistled, and you said "All change".'

'In between whiles I may have said "Chuff".'

'Just "Chuff"?'

'No, I believe I said "Chuff-Chuff". More lifelike, you know. The sound an engine makes when getting up steam.'

'Oh, playing trains!' Polly exclaimed. 'Did you say anything else?'

'There's a peculiar noise the carriages make going over the rails. It sounds more like "Duppidy-dee" than anything else.'

'So sometimes you said "Duppidy-dee"?'

'And then "Duppidy-dur. Duppidy-dee, duppidy-dur, duppidy-dee, duppidy-dur". Remarkable imitation, isn't it?'

'Remarkable,' agreed Polly. 'You ran, you all changed, you whistled, you chuffed, you duppidy-deed, duppidy-durred. Anything else?'

'I did have a small green flag to wave.'

'Is that all?'

'Somehow or other, in the past, I seem to have acquired a porter's cap,' said the wolf carefully.

'So you wore that?'

'And my sheriff's badge of course. It all adds to the effect.'

'And where was this remarkable performance, Wolf?' asked Polly.

'Here,' said the wolf simply. 'In the High Street.'

'And no one so much as looked at you?'

'Well of course there was a certain amount of sound effect,' the wolf admitted. 'And as I was invisible, no doubt some people were surprised to hear the – er – impressions of a train without there being anything to see.'

'So some notice was taken?'

'People looked in my direction, yes, but seeing nothing they were rather at a loss to explain what they heard. Their expressions of amazement were quite amusing.'

'Oh, my poor Wolf,' Polly exclaimed. 'You have made a fool of yourself. Of course they could see you –'

'They could not,' interrupted the wolf. 'I was invisible.'

'Wolf,' said Polly seriously, 'if you are invisible, can *anyone* see you?'

'Of course not.'

'Not even you yourself?'

'Naturally I couldn't.'

'Wolf,' said Polly gently. 'Just look down at the ground where your invisible feet are.'

The wolf looked down.

'Someone has left two very dirty paw marks there,' he said severely.

'They are your own paws, Wolf.'

'And those black things above – are they –?'

'They are your legs.'

The wolf stretched out first one paw and then the other and looked at them carefully. He turned round and scrutinized his tail. Then he squinted down and saw the end of his nose.

'Am I all visible, Polly?' he asked in a very small voice.

'All of you, Wolf.'

'Every single bit of me?'

'Everything, Wolf.'

'Do you mean they all saw me being a train? Did they see me shunting? Did they know it was me saying "Chuff-chuff"?'

'And "Duppidy-dee, duppidy-dur", Wolf.'

'I'll never be able to hold up my head here again,' said the wolf miserably. 'Making a public spectacle of myself in the street. I'll never be able to look a baby in the face from now on. It's all your fault, Polly. I'd never have tried to become invisible if I hadn't wanted to get you to eat. Never mind. Visible or invisible, I'll get you yet and then I shall be revenged.'

And Polly let him have the last word this time, as she felt rather sorry, as he went disconsolately away, for such a very, very visible wolf.

6. Huff, Puff

IT WAS a very calm and sunny day when Polly heard a most peculiar noise outside the house. It sounded like a small storm. She could hear the wind whistling round the corner of the house, but when she looked up at the treetops they were not even swaying; everything was perfectly still.

The noise stopped. Polly went on reading.

Suddenly it began again. The clean washing hung out at the back of the house blew about violently for a short time, but the treetops and clouds took no notice. It was very odd.

Again the noise stopped as suddenly as it had begun.

Polly went to the sitting-room window which looked out in front of the house, but she could see nothing. She went to the kitchen at the back of the house and looked out.

She saw the wolf. He was leaning against the garden wall and fanning himself with a large leaf off a plane tree. He looked hot and exhausted. As Polly looked, he stopped fanning, threw away the leaf, and began some extraordinary contortions.

First he bent himself double and straightened up again. Then he made one or two huge bites at nothing and appeared to swallow some large mouthfuls of air. Then he threw back his head and snorted loudly. Finally he bent double again and started to breathe in. As he breathed in he stood up and swelled out. He swelled and he swelled till from being a thin black wolf he became quite a fat black wolf, and his chest was as round as a barrel.

Then he blew.

'So that was the extraordinary noise,' Polly said to herself. She opened the kitchen window and leant out. The curtains blew about behind her in the wolf-made wind.

'What are you doing, Wolf?' she called out to him, as his breath gave out and the noise got less.

'Practising,' the wolf said airily. 'Just practising.'

'What for?'

'Blowing your house down, of course.'

'Blowing down this house?' Polly asked. 'This house? But you couldn't. It's much too solid.'

'It looks solid I admit,' the wolf said. 'But I know that's all sham. And if I go on practising I'll get plenty of push in my blow and then one day – Heigh presto! (that's what they always say in books),' he added, '– over it will topple and I shall eat you up.'

'But this is a brick house,' Polly objected.

'Well, I know it looks like brick, but it can't really be brick. It's mud really, isn't it now?'

'You're thinking of the Three Little Pigs,' said Polly. 'They built their houses of mud and sticks, the first two did, didn't they?'

'Well, yes I am,' the wolf admitted. 'But there's only one of you so I thought you'd probably build three houses. One of mud, and the next of sticks, and then a brick one.'

'This is the brick one,' said Polly firmly.

'Did you build the others first?' asked the wolf.

'No, I didn't. And I didn't build this one either. I just came to live in it.'

'You're sure it's not mud underneath that sort of brick pattern?' asked the wolf anxiously. 'Because when I was huffing and puffing just now, it seemed to me to give a sort of wobble. As if it might fall down some time if I blew hard enough.'

Polly felt a little frightened, but she was fairly sure the wolf couldn't blow down a brick house, so she said, 'Try again and let me see.'

The wolf doubled himself up, filled himself out and then blew with all his might. The blades of grass and the rose bushes and the clean washing waved madly in the wind, but the house never stirred at all.

'No,' said Polly, very much relieved. 'You aren't blowing down this house. It really is brick and I don't see why you should expect to be able to blow down a brick house. Even the wolf in the three little pigs' story couldn't do that. He had to climb down the chimney.'

'I thought if I practised long enough I might be able to,' the wolf said. 'After all, that incident with the pigs was a long time ago. We've probably learnt a lot about blowing since then. The wonders of Science, you know, and that sort of thing. Besides I had a book.'

From the grass beside him he picked up a small paper-covered volume and showed it to Polly. It was called *How to Become an Athlete*.

'An Ath what?' Polly asked, leaning even further out of the window.

'Good at games, that means,' the wolf explained. 'Wait a minute, there's a bit here . . .' He shuffled through the pages. 'Ah, yes, here we are. *Deep breathing. By constant practise of the following exercises, considerable respiratory power may be attained.*'

'What sort of power?'

'You can blow very hard. I've been doing the exercises for nearly a week and I can blow much harder than before.'

'But not hard enough to blow this house down,' Polly said.

'Don't you think, with some more practice –?' the wolf said hopefully.

'No,' said Polly. 'I don't.'

The wolf looked crestfallen for a moment, but then he cheered up again.

'Never mind,' he said quite gaily. 'If I can't blow it down with my breathing exercises I'll blow it down another way.'

'How?' asked Polly.

For answer the wolf dived behind some bushes and pulled out a large shabby suitcase. From inside the suitcase he produced a pair of bellows.

'Look,' he said proudly. 'This will do the trick. These bellows – wait a minute.'

He searched about in the suitcase and brought out a dirty piece of paper, which he unfolded and read.

'*These bellows are guaranteed to produce a wind equal to a gale of forty miles an hour if used properly*. Guaranteed, you see, Polly,' said the wolf, looking at her to see if she was impressed.

'But only if you use them properly,' Polly pointed out. 'Anyhow, how much is a gale of forty miles an hour?'

'A great lot,' the wolf assured her. 'A terribly strong wind. You could hardly stand up in it. In fact I shouldn't think you could stand up in it. And now,' he added, twirling the bellows

44

round and then pointing them at Polly, 'I am going to blow the house down.'

'Wait a minute,' said Polly, rather alarmed. 'I don't want the house to fall down on my head.'

She left the window and sat down on the floor under the kitchen table.

'Now I'm ready,' she called out. 'All right, Wolf.'

She heard the wolf spit on his paws before he picked up the bellows.

'I'll Huff,' he announced loudly and dramatically, 'and I'll Puff and I'll Blow your house down.'

There was a feeble little hiss of air, just the kind of noise a dying balloon makes. Then there was a silence.

'Perhaps you didn't use them properly,' Polly called out.

'I only know one way to use bellows,' the wolf said, very puzzled. 'Perhaps I didn't open them far enough.'

There was a cracking, tearing sound and Polly, as she came out from under the table, saw the wolf throw a pair of broken bellows over the garden wall.

'Guaranteed,' he muttered crossly to himself. 'I'll show them. I could make a better gale of forty miles an hour by blowing myself, with my head tied up in a bag. Bellows indeed.'

'Then you won't be able to blow the house down,' Polly said comfortably, seating herself on the window seat again.

'Oh, yes I shall,' said the wolf, fumbling in his suitcase again. 'I've got a thing here – it works by gunpowder, so it's awfully powerful. It'll blow the house down as soon as look at you.'

From the suitcase he produced something the size and shape of a small vegetable marrow, in a paper bag slightly too small for it.

'What is it?' Polly asked, very much interested.

'A bomb,' the wolf said casually. 'Just a small one, but it's supposed to be able to blow

up a small village or a large factory, so I should think it would about finish your little house, wouldn't you?'

He felt inside the paper bag and pulled out a sheet of closely printed pink paper.

'*Instructions*,' he read out. '*How to work the Wonder Bomb, and Guarantee for satisfactory results.*'

'Guarantee,' he snarled suddenly. He screwed the paper up and threw it over the wall.

'Now then,' he said. He held the paper bag upside down and shook it. 'Won't come out,' he said, puzzled.

'Oh, be careful,' Polly implored him. 'If you let that bomb drop it may go off and blow us all up.'

'I've got to get it out of the bag first,' the wolf complained. 'I can't see how it works until I get it out.'

He continued to shake the bag vigorously. Suddenly the paper tore, and the wolf just managed to catch the bomb as it fell.

'Now,' he said, smelling it doubtfully all round. 'Somewhere there must be something you have to do to get it to go off. The man in the shop did show me but I can't quite remember. A pin you pull out, I think, or push in, or something like that.'

'Oh, do be careful,' Polly said anxiously. She was terribly frightened, but it didn't seem much use to go and hide anywhere if the whole house was going to be blown up at any moment.

'Instructions,' the wolf said suddenly. 'There should be some instructions.'

He looked inside the torn paper bag. Then he looked in his suitcase. Then he looked at Polly. A moment later he was bounding over the garden wall in the direction in which he had thrown the crumpled ball of pink paper.

'Ow,' Polly heard from the other side of the wall. 'Ow. Wow! Ugh! Bother these nettles! Wow!'

The wolf climbed back into the garden. He sat down on the grass and licked his paws. He had no piece of pink paper.

'You grow a lot of nettles outside your garden,' he said crossly. 'And I can't find the instructions anywhere. I shall have to guess.'

He smelt the bomb again.

'There's a bit sticking out just here. Supposing I push it in?'

Polly summoned all her courage.

'All right,' she said, as calmly as she could. 'But you know the danger?'

'What?'

'If it makes the bomb go off at once –'

'It will blow your house up,' interrupted the wolf triumphantly.

'Yes, but it will blow us up too.'

'Us?'

'Me and you. There won't be much of me left for you to eat and there won't be any of you left to be interested in eating me.'

The wolf considered this.

'You mean I might be killed?'

'If that bomb goes off while you're holding it in your hand I shouldn't think there's the slightest chance of you living any longer than me.'

'Oh,' said the wolf. He held out the bomb to Polly. 'Here,' he said generously, 'you have it. I'll give it to you as a present. I haven't got the brains for this sort of thing. You have a look at it and see how it works. You're clever, you know, Polly. You'll soon find out how to make it go off.'

Polly shook her head.

'No, thank you, Wolf. I don't want to be blown up any more than you do.'

'Really?'

'Really. You put it back in your suitcase and take it somewhere a long way away from here and get rid of it.'

'Shall I give it to a little boy who is interested in how things work?' the wolf suggested, cautiously wrapping the bomb up in the remains of the too-small paper bag.

'No, that would be very dangerous.'

'Yes, I see what you mean,' the wolf agreed. 'He might make it go off before I was out of reach.'

'I think you'd better take it back to the shop you got it from,' Polly said. 'Now be careful, Wolf. Don't sling that suitcase about too much, unless you want to get blown to pieces.'

'I'll be very careful,' the wolf promised. He picked up the suitcase, holding the handle delicately in his teeth, and trotted towards the garden gate. Just before he went out he put the suitcase gently down and tilting back his head took a long look at the roof of Polly's house.

'Polly,' he called out. 'Polly! When were your chimneys last swept?'

Polly couldn't help laughing, but she answered very politely, 'About six months ago, I think, Wolf. Why do you want to know?'

'Oh, no particular reason,' said the wolf. 'I'm just interested in chimneys, that's all.'

'You must come and see ours sometime,' Polly said kindly. 'I'm afraid they're rather narrow and some of them are very twisty. And of course none of them are quite clean. Still, you could come and look from outside. Only you'll be careful of the boiling water, won't you? We always keep a pot of boiling water underneath the only big chimney, just in case anything we don't want comes down it.'

'Thank you, Polly,' said the wolf rather coldly. 'Most interesting. Another day, perhaps. Just at the moment I am rather busy.'

And picking up the suitcase handle in his mouth again, he went out of the garden gate and trotted, very slowly and carefully, down the road.

'I'm glad,' thought Polly, 'he didn't blow my house down. I only hope he won't go now and blow himself up.'

7. Monday's Child

POLLY was sitting in the garden making a daisy chain. She had grown her right thumb nail especially long on purpose to be able to do this, which meant that for the last two weeks she had said to her mother, 'Please don't cut the nail on that thumb, I need it long.' And her mother obligingly hadn't. Now it was beautifully long and only a little black. Polly slit up fat pink stalk after fat pink stalk. The daisy chain grew longer and longer.

As she worked, Polly talked to herself. It was half talking, half singing.

'Monday's child is fair of face,' she said. 'Tuesday's child is full of grace. Wednesday's child –'

'Is good to fry,' interrupted the wolf. He was looking hungrily over the garden wall.

'That's not right,' said Polly indignantly. 'It's Wednesday's child is full of woe, Thursday's child has far to go. There's nothing about frying in it at all.'

'There's nothing about woe, or going far in the poem I know,' protested the wolf. 'What would be the use of that?'

'The use?' Polly repeated. 'It isn't meant to be useful, exactly. It's just to tell you what children are like when they're born on which days.'

'Which days?' the wolf asked, puzzled.

'Well, any day, then.'

'But which is a Which Day?'

'Oh dear,' said Polly. 'Perhaps I didn't explain very well. Look, Wolf! If you're born on a Monday you'll be fair of face, because that is what the poem says. And if you're born on a Tuesday you'll be full of grace. See?'

'I'd rather be full of food,' the wolf murmured, 'I don't think grace sounds very satisfying.'

'And if you're born on a Wednesday you'll be full of woe,' said Polly, taking no notice of the interruption.

'Worse than grace,' the wolf said. 'But my poem's quite different. My poem says that Wednesday's child is good to fry. That's much more useful than knowing that it's full of woe. What good does it do anyone to know that? My poem is a useful poem.'

'Is it all about frying?' Polly asked.

The wolf thought for a moment.

'No,' he said presently. 'None of the rest of it is about frying. But it's good. It tells you the sort of thing you want to know. Useful information.'

'Is it all about cooking?' Polly asked severely.

'Well, yes, most of it. But it's about children too,' the wolf said eagerly.

'That's disgusting,' said Polly.

'It isn't, it's most interesting. And instructive. For instance, I can probably guess what day of the week you were born on, Polly.'

'What day?'

The wolf looked at Polly carefully. Then he looked up at the sky and seemed to be repeating something silently to himself.

'Either a Monday or a Friday,' he said at last.

'It was a Monday,' Polly admitted. 'But you could have guessed that from my poem.'

'What does yours say?' the wolf asked.

'Monday's child is fair of face, Tuesday's child is full of grace, and I am fair, in the hair anyway,' Polly said.

'Go on. Say the whole poem.'

Polly said:

'Monday's child is fair of face,
Tuesday's child is full of grace,

Wednesday's child is full of woe,
Thursday's child has far to go.
Friday's child is loving and giving,
Saturday's child works hard for its living.
But the child that is born on the
    Sabbath day
Is bonny and blithe and good and gay.'

'Pooh,' cried the wolf. 'What a namby-pamby poem! There isn't a single thing I'd want to know about a child in the whole thing. And, anyway, most of it you could see with half an eye directly you met the child.'

'You couldn't see that it had far to go,' Polly argued.

'No,' the wolf agreed. 'That's the best line certainly. But it depends how far it had to go, doesn't it? I mean if it had gone a long, long way from home you might be able just to snap it up without any fuss. But then it might be tough from taking so much exercise. Not really much help.'

'It isn't meant to be much help in the way you mean,' said Polly.

'And it isn't what I call a poem, either,' the wolf added.

'Why?' asked Polly. 'It rhymes, doesn't it?'

'Oh, rhymes,' said the wolf scornfully. 'Yes, if that's all you want. It jingles along if that satisfies you. No, I meant it doesn't make you go all funny inside like real poetry does. It doesn't bring tears to your eyes and make you feel you understand life for the first time, like proper poetry.'

'Is the poem you know proper poetry?' Polly asked suspiciously.

'Certainly it is,' the wolf said indignantly. 'I'll say it to you and then you'll see.

'Monday's child is fairly tough,
Tuesday's child is tender enough,
Wednesday's child is good to fry,
Thursday's child is best in pie.
Friday's child makes good meat roll,

Saturday's child is casserole.
But the child that is born on the Sabbath day,
Is delicious when eaten in any way.

'Now you can't hear that without having some pretty terrific feelings, can you?'

The wolf clasped his paws over his stomach and looked longingly at Polly.

'It gives me a queer tingling feeling in my inside,' he went on. 'Like a sort of beautiful, hungry pain. As if I could eat a whole lot of meals put together and not be uncomfortable afterwards. Now I'm sure your poem doesn't make you feel like that?'

'No, it doesn't,' Polly admitted.

'Does it make you feel anything?' the wolf persisted.

'No-o-o. But I like it. I shall have my children born on Sunday and then they'll be like what the poem says.'

'That would be nice,' agreed the wolf. 'But one very seldom gets a Sunday child. I believe they're delicious, even if you eat them without cooking at all!'

'I didn't mean to eat,' said Polly coldly. 'I meant children of my own. Bonny and blithe and all that.'

'What day did you say you were born on?' the wolf enquired. 'Did you say Monday or Friday?'

'Monday,' said Polly. 'Fair of face.'

'Fairly tough,' said the wolf thoughtfully to himself. 'Still, there's always steaming,' he added. 'Or stewing in a very slow oven. Worth trying, I think.'

He made a bound over the garden wall on to the lawn. But Polly had been too quick for him. She had run into the house and shut the door behind her before the wolf had recovered his balance from landing on the grass.

'Ah well,' sighed the wolf, picking himself up. 'These literary discussions! Very often don't get one anywhere. A tough proposition, this Polly. I'll concentrate on something tenderer and easier to get for today.'

And picking up the daisy chain, which Polly had left behind her, he wound it round his ears and trotted peacefully out of the garden and away down the road.

8. The Wolf in the Zoo

ONE DAY Polly was taken to the Zoo by her mother. She went to see the bears and the sea lions, the penguins and the camels. She saw the fishes and the monkeys and snakes and mice and tortoises. Then she saw the lions and the tigers, and she enjoyed it all very much.

'Now,' she said to her mother, 'I want to see the foxes and the wolves. I want to see if my Wolf is like other wolves.'

Her mother showed her where the cages were, but she said she would sit down and

wait for Polly, as she didn't want to go and see the foxes and wolves herself.

So Polly went over to the cages and looked at the foxes, who seemed to be asleep, and at a hyena who was awake, but cross. Then she moved on to look at the wolves.

In one cage there was a smallish wolf eating alone. In the next cage was a very large black wolf, exactly like the wolf Polly knew so well.

'But he is just like my Wolf!' Polly said in surprise.

'Hullo, Polly,' said the wolf in a gloomy voice. 'So you've found me at last, have you? How did you know I was here?'

'I didn't,' said Polly. 'It's an accident. I came over just to look at wolves. I never expected to find you here, Wolf.'

'Oh, dear, oh dear,' said the wolf. Two large tears dropped from his eyes on to the straw on the floor of his cage, and Polly felt rather sorry for him.

'How did you get here?' she asked. 'Did you come here on purpose, or did they catch you like the other animals?'

'The Other Animals!' the wolf said bitterly. His voice was choked with tears. 'Would I have come on purpose, do you think? Is it likely that I'd choose to live in this beastly little cage, where I've hardly room to turn round, when I might be outside, walking about the country and chasing you?'

'Well, I didn't know,' said Polly reasonably. 'You might have got tired of trying to catch little girls to eat and want to be fed for a change. They do feed you properly here, I suppose?' she added kindly.

'Bones,' said the wolf, sounding very sad. 'That's all. Bones. Hardly any meat on them. And raw. Think of that, Polly, for a wolf like me, that's been used to well-cooked meals, daintily served. Just bones, thrown into the cage, without so much as a sprig of parsley or a morsel of gravy with them. I could cry when I think of the meals you've cooked me, Polly, and I look at what they give you here –'

'But how did you get here, then?' Polly asked, still curious to know.

'There was an advertisement,' the wolf said. He sounded a little embarrassed. '"Wolf wanted," the advertisement said. "Large black wolf welcomed by fellows of Zoo something Society. Every care taken and suitable diet provided." So I came. It was the word Welcome that attracted me,' he added sadly.

'But didn't they?' Polly asked.

'If you call this Welcoming,' the wolf said, looking round his cage. 'I'd hardly set foot in the grounds and spoken to one of the keepers before there was such a hullabaloo as you've never heard. Men fetching chains, and others fetching ropes, and a sort of cage thing on wheels and me pushed into it as if I was a wild animal. Welcome, indeed!' The wolf snorted. Then a tear dropped from his eye again. 'If you knew how I want to be wanted,' he almost wept. 'I thought someone really wanted me at last. I'm large, aren't I? and black? and I'm a wolf. But if I'd been a snake they couldn't have been less welcoming.'

'Oh, poor Wolf,' said Polly. She was very nearly crying herself at this pathetic story.

'And if they think raw bones are a suitable diet, they've a lot to learn about wolves,' the wolf finished with a snarl.

'I've got a treacle toffee in my pocket,' Polly suggested. 'Would you like it?' She unwrapped it and pushed it through the bars. The wolf snapped it up so eagerly that Polly's fingers nearly disappeared too.

'No feeding the animals, Miss,' a friendly keeper advised her as he passed by. 'It's not safe. Treacherous beasts, wolves.'

The wolf gave a growl that made the keeper more certain than ever that he was a bad-tempered, untrustworthy animal. But Polly understood that he was angry because he was miserable, and though she didn't put her hand up to the bars again, she didn't move away.

'Wolf,' she whispered, when the keeper had passed out of sight. 'Perhaps I could bring you something nice to eat. What would you like best in the world?'

The wolf's eyes glistened and his tongue began to drip.

'A nice fresh juicy little girl,' he began. 'Fried, I think, with mushrooms and onions and perhaps a little –'

'Don't be silly,' Polly said sharply. 'You might know I'm not going to feed you on little

68

girls. Can't you think of something possible? Apple pie, for instance, or a Cornish pasty or fudge perhaps. Do you like fudge, Wolf?'

'I'd rather have a little g–' began the wolf, but as he caught Polly's eye he altered what he had been going to say.

'I'd like almost anything,' he admitted. 'Except bones. We get plenty of them here. But what I'd like best, Polly, if you could manage it, would be for you to get me out of here.'

'Out of your cage?' asked Polly. She looked doubtfully at the strong bars and the lock on the door. 'I don't think I could. I'm not strong enough to break the cage open, and I haven't got a key.'

'Of course you couldn't break it open,' said the wolf scornfully. 'I can't myself, so naturally you wouldn't be able to. But you could get a key, couldn't you? After all, you are Clever Polly, you know, so you ought to be able to think of some way of getting me out.'

'I'll think about it,' said Polly. She felt very sorry for the wolf, and yet rather suspicious of him. 'But how would I know you wouldn't start trying to eat me up again directly you came out?' she asked.

'You wouldn't know,' the wolf replied candidly. 'I might or I might not. It would depend on how I felt. You'd just have to wait and see.'

'Then I shan't do anything about you,' Polly said indignantly. 'I don't know why you should expect me to help you out just to eat me up.'

'Of course I should always be grateful,' the wolf assured her. 'I might be so grateful that I wouldn't want to eat you up. Please help me, Polly. If you don't nobody will, and I shall stay here for ever and ever until I am dead.'

Polly's kind heart was touched and she promised that she would at any rate bring the wolf something to eat and if possible think of a way of getting him out.

The next day Polly was very busy baking at home and the day after she brought the wolf a large Cornish pasty full of meat and onion and carrot and potato, nicely cooked and brown and shiny on top. She pushed it through the bars when the keeper was looking another way and watched anxiously to see what the wolf would do.

'Ah!' said the wolf. 'Pasty. My favourite first course.'

He swallowed the whole pasty at one gulp. Polly turned a little pale.

'Wolf,' she said, after a moment or two. 'Do you feel quite all right inside?'

'Better, thank you,' said the wolf. 'Pasty's a nice change after bones. Why?'

'I didn't mean you to eat it all in one gulp like that,' Polly began.

'That's all right, thank you, Polly. You don't know what good digestions we wolves have got. Why, I could swallow down a tender little morsel like you in about three bites, I should say, and as for a little pasty like that one – why it just slipped down without any trouble.'

'Yes, I daresay,' said Polly sadly. 'But it wasn't just an ordinary pasty.'

'Excellent,' declared the wolf, licking his chops.

'Yes, but it hadn't just got meat and vegetables in it.'

'A touch of garlic? A suspicion of chives?'

'It had a key in it.'

There was a short silence.

'Would the key have fitted the lock on the door of my cage?' the wolf asked casually.

'I think so,' Polly said. 'I went specially to a shop and asked for the sort of key that opens cage doors, and it looked all right.'

'So I should have been able to let myself out?'

'That was what I thought,' said Polly.

There was another short silence.

'Wow,' said the wolf suddenly. 'I've got an awful pain. In my – down here. It's hard and knobbly. It's got a sort of handle to it. I'll have to go and lie down.'

'I'll try again,' Polly said as she prepared to leave. 'But next time, Wolf, do for goodness' sake look before you eat whatever I send.'

Two days later a long thin parcel arrived for the wolf. He tore off the wrappings and inside was a stick of brightly coloured rock, with BRIGHTON written across the end. A suspicious keeper, who had come to make sure the parcel contained nothing contraband, smiled sourly as he saw the wolf studying the rock and left him with it, removing the brown paper and string.

'It's a message,' said the wolf to himself. 'I shall eat it very slowly and read the message as I go, and then I shall know how to escape.'

He licked busily at one end of the stick. After some time he had got rid of about an inch of rock, but the writing still said BRIGHTON.

'Funny,' thought the wolf. 'I'd better get through some more.'

But after half an hour's serious work, when there was only a piece the size of a sixpence left, the rock still said nothing but BRIGHTON.

'Maddening,' the wolf snarled, crunching the remaining bit up angrily. 'I was as careful as careful and it didn't make sense at all. At any rate, Polly can't tell me there was a key inside that miserable piece of rock, and if there was supposed to be a message all I can say is her spelling is very queer.'

When Polly arrived a week or so later she looked sadly at the wolf through the bars.

'So it went wrong again,' she said. 'I'd expected you to be out by now.'

'How could I get out?' the wolf asked crossly.

'I thought you'd have filed your way out. That stick of rock I sent you –'

'It didn't make sense,' the wolf grumbled. 'BRIGHTON it said all the way through and what use that is to me, I don't know.'

'Oh, you stupid animal,' Polly said, exasperated. 'The stick of rock was just to throw the keepers off the scent. The important thing in the parcel was the file – that was why it had to be a long thin parcel. I meant you to file through the bars to get out. I suppose you threw the file away with the paper and string.'

The wolf didn't answer this, but Polly could see that she had guessed right.

'Here's your last chance,' she said, handing over a small bottle with a closely printed label.

'And this time don't make any stupid mistakes, Wolf. I've got to go now, Mother's waiting for me.'

When she had gone the wolf considered the bottle carefully. It had no wrappings, so there couldn't be a file concealed there. He drew out the cork with his teeth and smelt the contents. Then he stuck a long red tongue down the neck of the bottle and tasted.

'Ah,' he said to himself. 'Very good. Sweet and strong. I'll drink it slowly, very slowly, and then I shall find out if it's got anything hidden inside.'

He drank.

When Polly saw the wolf walking quietly on a road near her home a few days later, she called out to him.

'Wolf! So you got out all right this time?'

'Yes,' said the wolf rather shortly, 'I got out.'

'You put the sleeping medicine in the keeper's cup of tea, I suppose?'

'No,' said the wolf uneasily. 'I didn't exactly do that.'

'In his pot of beer?'

'No.'

'In his tonic water?'

'As a matter of fact,' the wolf admitted, 'I didn't give it to him at all. I drank it myself.'

'But it said on the label –'

'I didn't read the label. Last time you sent me something with writing on it it wasn't any help, so this time I just drank the medicine to make sure there wasn't anything hidden in the bottle.'

'And what happened?'

'Well, I went to sleep. And I slept and I slept and I slept. So they thought I was dead and after about a day they didn't bother to lock the cage door. So I woke up and I came out. I just walked out, and here I am. And now,' said the wolf suddenly, 'I'm very, very hungry and I'm going to eat you up.'

But Polly ran. She ran like the wind, and
the wolf, who was stiff from being cramped in
his cage at the Zoo, and sleepy from his
sleeping medicine, couldn't run quickly
enough to catch her. So Polly got safely home
and the wolf didn't get her that time.

9. Polly Goes for a Walk

THE WOLF, you know, was determined to get Polly somehow, by hook or by crook, and Polly was determined not to be got.

One day, when Polly was out for a walk, she saw the wolf following her carefully and looking at every step she took.

'Now what's the matter, Wolf?' Polly asked impatiently. 'Why do you keep looking at my feet? I haven't got a hole in my socks, have I?'

'I'm not looking at your socks,' the wolf replied. 'I'm looking to see if you walk on one of the cracks in the pavement. As long as you walk on the squares you are safe, but if you walk on a line you are mine, and I shall gobble you up.'

Polly took great care how she trod. She always planted her feet firmly in the middle of each square. But presently she came to a little knot of people all standing outside the post-office, and as she passed, one of them moved quickly and knocked her off her balance. One of her feet went on to a line.

'Got you!' growled the wolf, coming up quickly behind her, ready to snatch her away.

'Wait a moment, Wolf,' said Polly. 'There must be two sides to an agreement. It's all very well for you to say I belong to you if I step on a line, but what do I get when you step on a line?'

'What do you mean?' asked the wolf uncomfortably. He hadn't been looking at all where he put his paws.

'Well,' said Polly, 'if you are to get me to eat if I step on a line, I think it's only fair that I should be allowed to eat you if you step on a line. Don't you?'

'Well yes, I suppose it is,' the wolf agreed reluctantly.

'Well, I've stepped on one line, because I was pushed, but you've stepped on lots, and all because you were careless. Now how about it, Wolf?'

'We'd better begin again,' the wolf said in a great hurry. 'We'll begin from when I say *now*. One, two, three . . . *now*!'

But Polly was careful not to step on any more lines that day, and she reached home safely.

The next day she went for a walk on the heath and presently she noticed the wolf following her again.

'Touch wood,' the wolf called to her, between the trees. 'As long as you are touching wood you are safe, but directly you aren't, I can come and get you.'

Polly ran from tree to tree; several times the wolf made a dash at her when she was between two trees, but she managed just to reach the next tree in time. All the time she was getting nearer and nearer home, but at last she had got to the edge of the heath and to reach home she had to go down the road where there weren't any trees at all.

'Aha!' said the wolf, 'now I've got you. You can't touch wood down that road so you will be mine.'

Polly looked up and down the road, but she couldn't see anyone in sight. It seemed as if she might have to stand holding on to the last tree for ever.

Then she had a good idea. She broke a twig off the side of the tree and held it out to the wolf.

'Animal, Vegetable or Mineral?' she asked him.

'Vegetable, of course,' said the wolf, puzzled.

'What's it made of?' asked clever Polly.

'Wood,' said the wolf, 'silly!'

'Well, I'm touching it,' said Polly, leaving the tree and walking slowly down the road towards her home, with the twig held firmly in her hand.

For several days Polly was very cautious about going out by herself, but at last her mother asked her to go and post a letter in the pillar box at the end of the road, and Polly set off with the letter in her hand.

She was just reaching up to put the letter through the slot, when the wolf jumped out from behind the pillar box.

'Aha!' he said, his red tongue hanging out. 'Now I've really got you.'

Polly thought quickly. She had almost let the letter fall through the slot, but now she held on to it.

'Listen, Wolf,' she said. 'Why do you think I came out here?'

'For a little breath of fresh air?' suggested the wolf.

'No. Try again,' said Polly.

'To meet me,' said the wolf, his eyes glistening.

'Not even that,' said Polly. 'Look at my hand. Not that one, silly, the one at the letter box.'

'To post a letter!' said the wolf in surprise.

'Right at last,' said Polly. 'And do you know who this letter is from and whom it's to? It's from my mother to the man who manages the Society for the Prevention of Cruelty to Children, and it's telling him to come and fetch you and take you away and put you in a

cage and lock you up for ever and ever because you've eaten me up. You won't like that, will you, Wolf?'

'No,' said the wolf, rather downcast. 'I shan't like it at all.'

Then he cheered up.

'But when I've eaten you up I'll eat up the letter too and then no one will ever know,' he said.

'But the letter is almost posted,' Polly said. 'My hand is holding it inside the pillar box, and the moment you touch me I shall let go and it will be posted.'

'Oh, please don't post it, Polly,' the wolf begged. 'Take it back and get your mother to alter it for me. Ask her to say that I've promised not to eat any other little girls, so I needn't be locked up for more than a week or so.'

'But how can I take it back, or get her to alter it if you've already eaten me up?' asked Polly.

The wolf thought. Then he said sadly, 'Perhaps I'd better not eat you *this* time, Polly, so that you can take the letter back and get it altered. But *next* time, Polly, you shan't get away so easily, so *look out*.'

But clever Polly smiled to herself, as she posted her mother's letter to an aunt in the country in a different pillar box that afternoon. For she had beaten the wolf again.

10. The Seventh Little Kid

POLLY was alone in the house, not for the first time, when the front doorbell rang. Being, after her earlier experiences, rather cautious, she did not open the door straight away, but lifted the letter-box lid and tried to peep through.

'Who is there?' she called out.

'Your mother, my dear,' said a harsh and familiar voice. 'Come back from shopping, with a present for you.'

'You don't sound at all like my mother,' Polly said suspiciously. She couldn't see much

through the letter box, and what she could
see didn't help. 'Say that again.'

'Your mother, my dear,' said the voice again,
'with something nice for you.'

'Why?' asked Polly, interested in spite of
herself.

'Why, what?' said the voice impatiently.

'Why with something nice for me. I mean,
specially? It isn't my birthday.'

'Oh bother,' said the voice very cross and
harsher than ever. 'Why do you want to say

all that? I don't know. Just to get you to open the door, of course.'

'Oh, go away, Wolf,' said Polly. 'I know it's you. Your voice is all wrong for my mother. She's got a nice soft voice and you sound like a – well, like a wolf. Of course I shan't open the door, you'd only eat me up.'

The wolf padded away down the front doorsteps without any difficulties. But a week or so later, when Polly was again alone in the house, the front doorbell rang again.

'Who is it, please?' called Polly through the letter box.

'Yourmothermydearcomebackfrom shoppingwithsomethingniceforeachofyou,' said the wolf very quickly, in a high sweet voice quite unlike his own.

'Oh,' said Polly. She knew quite well it wasn't her mother, who had in fact gone out to tea with a friend.

'It's early closing day,' she said. 'How did you manage to do any shopping?'

There was a silence. Then the wolf said, 'I went somewhere else where it wasn't early closing day.'

'What have you brought for me?' Polly asked, laughing to herself.

'Don't ask silly questions,' the wolf said angrily, but still in his false voice. 'I told you it was something nice.'

'Why don't you use your own front-door key and let yourself in?' Polly asked.

'I – I – I left it at home,' said the wolf. 'Don't keep on talking so much, I can't keep this plum stone in my mouth all the time without making my tongue sore.'

'What is the plum stone doing in your mouth?' Polly asked with interest.

'Making my voice higher and sweeter of course. I should have thought you could hear that. Go on, Polly, you haven't asked to see my hand.'

'Let me see your hand, Wolf?' said Polly obligingly. The wolf put up to the letter box a long black paw and at once started off down the front doorsteps.

'Hi!' said Polly. 'Why are you going? Don't you want me to open the door any more?'

'Oh yes, I want you to,' the wolf said, turning back. 'But of course you won't this time. First you know me because of my voice, and the next time you know me because of my black hand, but the third time you let me in and I gobble you up. Haven't you read about the Seven Little Kids, Polly?'

'I think I have,' Polly said. 'It's about a wolf, isn't it?'

'Yes, and he eats them all up but one,' said the wolf gloatingly. 'Just think! Five little kids, all to himself! No one to share with! All for him!'

'Six,' said Polly. 'One away from seven leaves six, not five, Wolf.'

'Better and better,' sighed the wolf. 'Anyway, I'll be back some time, Polly, in full disguise, and then it will all come right, you'll see.'

When he had gone Polly found the fairytales book with the story of the wolf and the seven little kids in it, and read it carefully. It seemed that if a wolf ever did come into the house, the clock case was the only safe place to hide in.

But a day or two later, when Polly's mother really had gone shopping and really had also forgotten her keys, a voice called from outside the door, 'Polly! I've forgotten my key, and I've got a very heavy basket. Come and open the door for me will you please!'

'Oh no!' said clever Polly, very much pleased with herself. 'No you don't. I know who you are and I won't open the door on any account.'

'Hurry up,' urged the voice, 'I'm nearly dropping a bag full of eggs and the basket handle is cutting my arm.'

'Go away, Wolf,' said Polly. 'I'm busy and I don't want to play this morning.'

'Polly!' said the voice angrily. 'Open the door for goodness' sake or . . .'

There was a loud smashing noise. Polly ran upstairs and looked out of a window. On the doorstep stood her mother, looking very cross, and at her feet was the remains of a dozen large eggs.

Polly ran down again and let her in.

'I've got to go out again,' her mother said, when she had unloaded her shopping basket. 'I still haven't finished my shopping. And if I ask you to let me in again, don't keep me waiting so long,' she added as she left.

So next time the front door bell rang, without waiting to ask any questions or even to look out, Polly ran to open the door. And in stepped the wolf, wearing two pairs of white gloves.

Polly did not stop to admire the gloves. She ran as quickly as she could into the sitting-room and climbed into the clock case.

The wolf came in a leisurely way after her, straight to the clock case, opened the little door and stood looking at Polly cowering inside.

'Come out,' he said, in the high sweet voice. 'Bother this plum stone!' He spat it out and added in his ordinary voice, 'That's better. Come out.'

Polly was frightened, but she was not going to give in so easily.

'Are you going to eat me up, Wolf?' she asked.

'I certainly am.'

'Like the seventh little kid?'

'Just like the seventh little kid, only I shall enjoy you more because I haven't had six to eat already.'

'Wolf,' said Polly. 'Did you read the rest of that story?'

'I read up to where he ate the six little kids,' said the wolf. 'I wasn't interested in what happened after that.'

'So you don't know what happened to that wolf? And what will happen to you if you eat me?'

'No,' the wolf said uneasily. 'Must you tell me now? Make it short, I'm terribly hungry.'

'I'll be as quick as I can,' Polly promised. 'But I think you ought to know what you're letting yourself in for. The mother goat knew, of course, what had happened to her kids, so she found the wolf when he was asleep and she cut him open with her big scissors and got the kids out of his stomach and sewed him up again with six big stones inside.'

'Wow,' the wolf exclaimed.

'Of course she gave him an anaesthetic?' he suggested a moment later. 'Something so that he didn't feel anything?'

'I don't believe so,' Polly answered.

'I wonder if the wound hurt afterwards,' the wolf pondered.

'I expect it did like anything,' Polly agreed.

'Has your mother any big scissors?' the wolf asked casually.

'Enormous ones. She uses them for cutting out our frocks generally.'

'And needles and thread?'

'Very big needles for sewing carpets and that tough thread – all hairy and hard.'

'And I can't be sure never to go to sleep,' the wolf said under his breath. 'Well, goodbye, Polly,' he went on aloud. 'It's been so nice seeing you. Remember me to your mother. I'm afraid I can't stay till she gets back. And you can come out of that clock case,' he called back as he reached the front door. It slammed behind him.

From the other side of it came the sound of someone licking the doorstep.

'Eggs,' Polly heard the wolf say to himself. 'Not very well cooked. Funny place to fry eggs, a doorstep. Still it's better than nothing. Thoughtful of them to have left them there, as I can't have Polly herself.'

11. In the Wolf's Kitchen

POLLY had been very careful for a long time not to give the wolf a chance of catching her. But perhaps she got a little careless, for one day she had hardly got outside the house before the wolf had caught her up in his mouth and run away with her. He took her into his house, locked the door behind them, and said:

'Now, Polly, I've really got you at last, and this time all your cleverness won't help you, for I am going to gobble you up.'

'Oh very well,' said Polly obligingly. She looked round. 'Where is the kitchen?' she asked.

'The kitchen?' said the wolf.

'But of course, the kitchen,' Polly said. 'You are going to cook me, aren't you? Oh, Wolf,' she said, as she looked at his surprised face, 'you can't mean that you were going to eat me raw?'

'No, no, of course not,' said the wolf, hastily. 'I shouldn't think of it. Of course I'm going to cook you. The kitchen is here, along this passage. But I'm afraid it's rather dark and rather – well, not quite as clean as it might be.'

'Never mind,' said Polly, following him, 'I daresay that won't bother me.'

The kitchen was very dark and very dirty. The windows were covered with soot and cobwebs, the floor had not been swept for days, and all the cups and plates needed washing. It was a terrible sight.

'Oh, dear,' said Polly, as she looked round. 'You certainly need someone to do a little housework here, Wolf. Now let's think what we are going to eat for lunch today, and then while you go out and do the shopping, I'll see if I can make this look a little better.'

'We needn't think about what we are going to eat,' snarled the wolf, 'because I am going to eat *you*!'

'Oh, Wolf,' said Polly sadly, 'how terribly impatient you are. Just feel my arm and see if I'm ready to be eaten yet.' She stuck out her elbow.

The wolf felt Polly's elbow and shook his head.

'Bony,' he said. 'Very disappointing. And you always looked such a nice solid little girl.'

'I'd make a much better meal for you if you fattened me up a bit first,' Polly assured him.

'If you expect me to go out catching little boys and girls for you to get fat on, you're very much mistaken,' the wolf said indignantly.

'No, no,' said Polly, 'I don't. All I suggest is that I should stay here for a little and try to get fat on my own cooking. Of course I should cook for you as well,' she added. 'And you know I cook quite nicely.'

'I remember,' said the wolf drily.

'Well then, won't you go out and get some carrots and potatoes, and some rashers of bacon, and perhaps tomatoes and mushrooms? And I'll make a stew for today,' said Polly.

The wolf grumbled a little, but at last he went out with a large market basket, locking the front door behind him. While he was gone Polly scrubbed the kitchen table and the floor. She lit the fire, and swept the hearth, she washed all the dishes and polished the saucepans till they winked. The only thing she couldn't do was to get the windows quite clean, because as she was locked in she couldn't wash the outsides. When the wolf came back he found the kitchen still rather dark, but spotless and shining. Polly peeled the potatoes, while the wolf sliced up onions and carrots, and presently a pot was simmering over the fire, sending out the most delicious smells.

'Mm-mm-mm,' said the wolf greedily a little later. 'Very good, this stew. This ought to fatten you up, Polly. Have some more, and mop up your gravy with a big hunk of bread.'

'I couldn't eat any more, thank you,' said Polly politely. 'But there is a little more for you, Wolf, if you can manage it.'

The wolf held out his plate and gobbled up his third helping. It was too dark for him to see how very little Polly had really eaten, and he felt full and comfortable and certain that on this sort of food Polly would soon be plump enough to eat.

After the meal the wolf fell asleep and slept soundly till the next morning. Then he felt Polly's arm again to see if she was ready to be eaten yet.

'Still disgustingly bony,' he said snappishly.

'Never mind,' said Polly. 'There's no hurry. Today, Wolf, we'll have cheese pudding and sultana roll. Here is a list of what you'll have to buy and while you are out, I'll go on cleaning the house.'

'Are cheese pudding and sultana roll fattening?' asked the wolf suspiciously.

'Very,' said Polly. 'Why, my grandma never eats them because she is trying to get thinner, but people who want to get fat eat almost nothing but sultana roll.'

So the wolf went out and did the shopping – but he remembered to lock the door behind him. And when he came back Polly made cheese pudding and sultana roll, and again at dinner Polly ate very little and the wolf ate a great deal, and went to sleep afterwards, and dreamt of Polly pudding and Polly roll, in happy, greedy dreams.

The next day the wolf felt Polly's arm and it was still very bony.

'Today,' he said, 'you had better cook something really solid. I can't wait much longer, and I don't believe you are getting fatter at all. I believe you cheated me when you said yesterday's meal was fattening.'

'All right,' said Polly. 'We'll have toad-in-the-hole and pancakes.'

'Pancakes!' said the wolf joyously. Then he added, in a suspicious voice, 'I don't like toads. They don't taste at all nice.'

'No, no,' said Polly. 'Not real toad. Sausages. In batter. Very good, and very filling.'

So for lunch they had toad-in-the-hole and pancakes. Polly ate two mouthfuls of toad-in-the-hole, and one small pancake, but the wolf ate a meat tin full of toad,

and eleven pancakes, thick with sugar.
Afterwards he was too full to go up to bed,
but slept in the kitchen, with his feet on the
mantelpiece.

The next morning he was very cross. He
felt Polly's elbow and growled at her.

'You're only skin and bone still,' he said.
'You're not worth the trouble I've been to to
catch you. Why aren't you getting fat? I'm
getting fatter since you've been here. Why
aren't you?'

'I don't know,' said Polly, pretending to look very sad. 'I was much fatter than this at home.'

'Are you cooking properly?' asked the wolf. 'Just like your mother cooks?'

'I thought I was,' said Polly. 'But there must be something wrong about what I do. Perhaps I've left something out, or put in something wrong.'

'Think,' the wolf urged her. 'Think hard. I can't wait much longer, and you don't seem to be getting any fatter.'

Polly thought. Then she shook her head.

'It's no good,' she said. 'Whatever it is I can't think of it.'

'Wouldn't your mother know?' asked the wolf.

'Now that's really a good idea,' said Polly, '*Clever* Wolf to think of that. I'll go home and ask my mother what I've been doing wrong, and then when she has told me, I can cook so as to make me fat enough for you to eat.'

'Go home quickly, then,' said the wolf, unlocking the front door, 'and ask your mother from me to tell you how to cook good fattening meals. Don't let her forget anything and don't you forget this time. Hurry up, Polly, I can't wait till you come back.'

And Polly did hurry up, and perhaps the wolf is still waiting, for she ran home and never went back to the wolf's kitchen again.

12. The Wolf in Disguise

'Now,' SAID the wolf to himself one day just before Christmas, 'I really must catch that Polly. I've tried This and I've tried That, and I've never managed to get her yet. What can I do to make sure of her this time, and get my Christmas dinner?'

He thought and thought and then he had a good idea.

'I know!' he exclaimed. 'I'll disguise myself. Of course the trouble before has always been that Polly could see I was a wolf. Now I'll dress up as a human being and Polly won't have any idea that I am a wolf until I have gobbled her up.'

So the next day the wolf disguised himself as a milkman and came round to Polly's house with a float full of milk bottles.

'Milk-oh!' he called out. But the door did not open.

'Milk-OH!' said the wolf louder.

'Just leave the bottles on the doorstep, please,' said Polly's voice from the window.

'I don't know how much milk you want today,' said the wolf. 'You'd better come and tell me.'

'Sorry, I can't,' said Polly. 'I'm on top of a ladder, hanging up Christmas decorations, and I can't come down just now. I've left a note saying how much milk I want in one of the empty bottles.'

Sure enough, there was the note. The wolf looked at it and left two pints, as it said, and then went off, very cross. Being a milkman was no good, he could see.

Polly wouldn't open the door just for a milkman.

A day or two later there was a knock on the door of Polly's house, and there on the doorstep stood a large, dark butcher, with a blue stripy apron and a wooden tray of meat over his shoulder. He rang the bell.

A window over the front door was opened, and a head all white with soap-suds looked out.

'Who is that?' asked Polly's voice. 'I can't open my eyes or the soap will get into them.'

'It's the butcher,' replied the wolf. 'With a large juicy piece of meat for you.'

He had decided that Polly certainly wouldn't be able to resist a piece of meat.

'Thank you,' said Polly. 'I'll be down in a minute or two. I've just got to finish having my hair washed and then I'll come down and open the door.'

The wolf was delighted. In a minute or two Polly would open the door and he would really get her at last. He could hardly wait.

His mouth began to water as he thought about it, and he felt terribly hungry.

'She is being a long time,' he thought. 'I'm getting hungrier and hungrier. I wonder how long hair-washing takes?'

He had put his meat tray down on the doorstep while he waited, and now he looked longingly at the piece of meat on the tray. It was juicy, and very tempting.

'She doesn't know how large it is,' he said to himself. 'She would never miss one bite off it.'

So he took one bite. It was delicious, but it made him hungrier still.

'I'm sure more than two minutes have gone,' he thought. 'I'll have to have another bite to keep myself going.'

His second bite was larger than his first.

'Really, it isn't worth leaving just that little bit,' he said, as he swallowed down the last bit of meat. 'Polly will never know whether I've got the meat or not. I'll keep the tray up where

she can't see it and she'll think the meat is still there.'

He hoisted the tray on to his shoulder. Just at that moment Polly looked out of the window again.

'Sorry to be so long,' she called out. 'Mother would give me a second soaping. And please, Butcher, she says, is it frying steak or stewing steak?'

'Oh – both!' said the wolf quickly. 'Either,' he added.

'But where is it?' asked Polly. 'Just now when I looked out I saw a great piece of meat on your tray, but now it isn't there!'

'Not there! Good heavens!' said the wolf. 'Some great animal must have eaten it while I was looking the other way.'

'Oh dear,' said Polly, 'so you haven't any meat for us, then?'

'No, I suppose I haven't,' said the wolf sadly.

'Well, I shan't come to the door, then,' said Polly, 'and anyhow I've got to have my hair dried now. Next time you come you'd better make sure no one eats the meat before you deliver it to us, Butcher.'

When he got home again the wolf thought and thought what he could take to the door of Polly's house that she wouldn't be able to resist and that he could.

Suddenly he knew. He would be a postman with a parcel. Polly couldn't possibly refuse to open the door to a postman with a parcel for her, and as long as the parcel did not contain meat, he himself would not be tempted.

So a few days later a Wolf postman rang the bell at Polly's door. In his hand he held a large brown paper parcel, addressed to Polly.

For a long time no one answered the door. Then the flap of the letter box lifted up from inside and Polly's voice said, 'Who is it?'

'The postman,' said the wolf, as carelessly as he could, 'with a parcel for someone called Polly.'

'Oh! Will you leave it on the doorstep, please,' said Polly.

'No, I can't do that,' said the wolf. 'You must open the door and take it in. Post-office regulations.'

'But I'm not allowed to open the door,' said Polly. 'My mother thinks that a wolf has been calling here lately, and she has told me not to open the door to anyone unless she is there too, and she's not here, so I can't.'

'Oh, what a pity,' said the wolf. 'Then I shall have to take this lovely parcel away again.'

'Won't you bring it another day?' asked Polly.

'No, there won't be time before Christmas,' said the wolf, very much pleased with himself.

'Well, perhaps it isn't anything I want anyway,' said Polly, comforting herself.

'Oh but it is,' said the wolf quickly. 'It's something very exciting, that you'd like very much.'

'What is it?' asked Polly.

'I don't think I ought to tell you,' said the wolf primly.

'How do you know what it is?' asked Polly. 'If you're really a postman you ought not to know what's inside the parcels you carry.'

'Oh – but it's – it's – a talking bird,' said the wolf. 'I heard it talking to itself inside the parcel.'

'What did it say?' asked Polly.

'Oh – "tweet, tweet", and things like that,' replied the wolf.

'Oh, just bird talk. Then I don't think I want it,' said Polly. She was beginning to be a little suspicious.

'Oh no,' said the wolf hastily. 'It can say words too. It says "Mum" and "Dad", and "Pretty Polly",' he added.

'It sounds lovely,' said Polly. 'But can it talk to you? I only want a bird who can carry on a conversation.'

'Oh yes, we had ever such a long talk coming up the hill,' the wolf assured her.

'What did you talk about?' asked Polly.

'Well, the weather,' said the wolf, 'and how hungry it makes us. And about Christmas dinner. And – and – the weather – and being very hungry.'

'What did the bird say it ate?' asked Polly.

The wolf was beginning to enjoy himself. Obviously Polly was interested now, and at any moment she would open the door to be given the parcel, and then he would be able to gobble her up.

'The bird said it ate gooseberries and chocolate creams,' he said, inventing wildly. 'So then I said I wouldn't like that at all. Not solid enough for me, I said. Give me a juicy little g–' he stopped himself just in time.

'A juicy little what?' asked Polly.

'A juicy little grilled steak,' said the wolf hastily.

'And what did the bird say then?'

'He said, "Well, that may be all very well for a wolf"–'

'Oho!' said Polly. 'So that's what you are! Not a postman at all, nothing but a wolf. Now listen, Wolf. Go away, and take your parcel, which I don't want, because it isn't a bird in a cage or anything like it, and don't come back either in your own skin or dressed up as anyone else, because whatever you do, *I shan't let you catch me, now or ever. Happy Christmas, Wolf.*' She shut the letter-box lid.

So the wolf did not get his Christmas dinner after all.

13. A Short Story

OUTSIDE Polly's house the lawn was white with daisies in the spring, and one day Polly, looking out of the window, saw the wolf, sitting on the grass busily taking the petals one by one, off a daisy. He was muttering to himself.

Polly leaned a little further, and rather dangerously, out of the window to listen. He wasn't saying, 'She loves me, she loves me not,' as you or I might, but, 'I get her, I don't get her, I get her, I don't get her.'

'Bother,' he ended suddenly, throwing away a stalk with no petals left on it. Obviously he had not got the answer he wanted. He picked another flower and started again.

'I get her,' he announced loudly, looking up at the house triumphantly, as he came to the end of his daisy.

'Oh no you don't,' said Polly. 'I saw you take off two petals together and count them as one. Cheating, Wolf, that is, and very unfair.'

'I didn't think anyone was looking,' the wolf said. 'You must have terribly good eyesight to be able to see from there.'

'I have,' said Polly. 'But even if I hadn't you ought not to cheat. You don't deserve to get anyone or anything if you cheat because no one is looking.'

'So you don't think I shall get you then?' the wolf asked, disappointed.

'Not on that daisy,' Polly answered.

'On the others?' the wolf asked hopefully.

'If you do them all,' Polly answered decidedly.

'Do you mean I've got to do the whole lot?' the wolf said in despair. He looked round the lawn. 'Why, there are hundreds here,' he protested. 'It would take me years to take the petals off all of them.'

'But you'll never know if you're going to get me or not unless you do,' Polly insisted.

'But by the time I've finished these daisies there'll probably be some more coming up.'

'It will keep you rather busy,' Polly admitted. 'But I expect you'll get through quite a lot if you stick to it. Besides you'll get quicker in time. Practice, you know,' she said encouragingly.

'But my paws are so clumsy,' the wolf protested. 'It isn't as if I had neat little hands like you.'

'You've quite nice paws, for a wolf,' Polly said kindly.

'You wouldn't like to help me, I suppose?' the wolf asked hopefully.

'No thank you,' said Polly. 'I've got quite a lot of other things I want to do.'

'If I get through all these daisies,' said the wolf, 'and it ends up that I'm going to get you at last, will you agree to come along quietly, without any fuss?'

Polly looked round the lawn. There were hundreds, probably thousands of daisies. But then the wolf might get really quick at taking the petals off. Or he might cheat.

'This isn't all the daisies in the world, Wolf,' Polly pointed out.

'Oh but surely there are enough here?' the wolf almost wailed.

'Quite enough,' Polly said. 'But, of course, you'll never know if it's the truth until you've got to the last daisy. And of course I couldn't agree to be eaten quietly, without any fuss, if I didn't know it was the truth.'

'You mean, I've got to unpick all the daisies there are, anywhere, everywhere?' cried the wolf.

'And when you get to the very last, if it says you are going to get me, I'll come,' said clever Polly. 'You can start here,' she added. 'There are a nice lot here to begin with.'

So the wolf spends his time picking daisies on Polly's lawn, and as there are plenty of daisies in the world, Polly thinks it will be a long time before he finds out whether or not he will ever get her. A Very Long Time.

A PUFFIN BOOK

Extra!

Extra!

READ ALL ABOUT IT!

CATHERINE STORR

CLEVER
POLLY
AND THE STUPID

1913	Born Catherine Cole on 21 July in Kensington, London
1924–31	Catherine is a pupil at St Paul's Girls' School in London where she is lucky enough to be taught by Gustav Holst, the music teacher at the school, learning to play the piano and the organ, eventually becoming the organist for the daily morning service at the school
1931	Catherine is accepted at Newnham College, Cambridge, where she studies English literature
1937	Catherine writes her first children's story, Ingeborg and Ruthy. Ruthy was the name of her much-loved doll as a child
1940	Ingeborg and Ruthy is published by George G. Harrap & Co. Catherine returns to Cambridge

to study medicine. At Cambridge she meets and falls in love with Anthony Storr, a fellow medical student

1942 *Catherine and Anthony marry*

1944 *Catherine and Anthony qualify as doctors. Both also start training in psychiatry. Catherine gives birth to the first of three daughters1950–63 Catherine works part-time as a senior medical officer in the Department of Psychological Medicine at the Middlesex Hospital and also writes stories for children. As her daughters grow older, she writes books for older children*

1952 *Her first two books are published:* Stories for Jane *and* Clever Polly, and other stories

1955 Clever Polly *and the* Stupid Wolf *is published and becomes hugely popular*

1957 *A sequel,* Polly and the Wolf Again, *is published*

1958 Marianne Dreams, *a novel for older children, is published. It has has remained in print ever since and has been published in many foreign languages*

1960 Marianne and Mark *(the sequel to* Marianne Dreams*) is published*

1961 *Catherine helps to set up the Charlotte M. Yonge Society, devoted to studying the Victorian novelist who was a bestselling author of her time*

1966 *Takes on a new job as an editor at Penguin Books and continues writing*

1971 Thursday, *a novel for young adults, is published*

2001 *Catherine dies aged eighty-seven on 8 January in London; her last book is published in the autumn*

INTERESTING FACTS

From very early childhood it was always Catherine's ambition to become a writer. She wrote over forty books for children and many novels, plays and works of non-fiction for adults.

Catherine had three daughters, Sophia, Polly and Emma.

Clever Polly and the Stupid Wolf has remained in print ever since its first publication in 1955.

Marjorie-Ann Watts comes from a very creative family. Her father was a graphic artist and a cartoonist for a magazine called Punch, *and both her mother and grandmother were writers. Marjorie-Ann trained as a painter and illustrator at the Chelsea School of Art in London, and worked as an art editor and typographer before writing and illustrating her own books for children. She has also written a novel and a guide to European painting for young people.*

INTERESTING FACT

When she illustrated the Clever Polly stories, Marjorie-Ann used Catherine Storr's daughter Polly as a model   so the drawings in this book are of the real Polly!

WHERE DID THE STORY
COME FROM?

*The first Clever Polly book was written by Catherine Storr
for her own daughter, Polly, who was frightened by wolves
and believed there was one hiding under her bed. The
story talks about Polly's fears and then dispels them in a
humorous way. The story became the inspiration for more
stories about Clever Polly and the Stupid Wolf, which have
reassured and entertained many other children, too.*

GUESS
WHO?

A   'I have planted a pip of a grape. This pip will grow into a vine and the vine will climb up the house and I shall climb up the vine.'

B   'I don't want my nice little Polly eaten up by a wolf.'

C   'I know who you are and I won't open the door on any account.'

D   'It's not safe. Treacherous beasts, wolves.'

WORDS GLORIOUS WORDS!

Lots of words have several different meanings – here are a few you'll find in this Puffin book. Use a **dictionary** or look them up online to find other definitions.

crestfallen *sad and disappointed*

disconsolately *hopelessly unhappy*

implore *to beg someone desperately*

indignantly *showing anger at what is seen as unfair treatment*

plaintively *sounding sad and mournful*

sheepish *feeling embarrassment from shame or lack of self-confidence*

scrutinize *examine or inspect closely*

DID YOU KNOW?

Wolves only go *hunting* when they are *hungry*, and can wander around for eight to ten hours a day *looking for prey.*

Wolves tend to mate for life, *and they are* devoted *parents.*

A wolf puppy's eyes are blue *when they are first born. Their eyes* turn yellow *by the time they are eight months old.*

QUIZ

Thinking caps on – let's see how much you can remember! Answers are at the bottom of the opposite page. (No peeking!)

1 *How many slices of chocolate cake does the wolf eat in* **Clever Polly***?*

a) *Two slices*

b) *Four slices*

c) *Six slices*

d) *He doesn't eat any chocolate cake*

2 *What does the wolf pull out of his suitcase in 'Huff, Puff' to help him blow Polly's house down?*

a) *Bellows*

b) *A book called* How to Become an Athlete

c) *A wind machine*

d) *A fan*

3 *What does the wolf say about Wednesday's child in 'Monday's Child'?*

a) *Wednesday's child has far to go*

b) *Wednesday's child is full of woe*

c) *Wednesday's child is best in pie*

d) *Wednesday's child is good to fry*

4 *What is the first thing that Polly gives the wolf to help him escape in 'The Wolf in the Zoo'?*

a) *A spade*

b) *A key*

c) *A file*

d) *Sleeping medicine*

5 *Who does Polly tell the wolf she is posting a letter to in 'Polly Goes for a Walk'?*

a) *Her aunt*

b) *The animal pound*

c) *The manager of the Society for the Prevention of Cruelty to Children*

d) *Her best friend*

MAKE AND DO

*Bake your own **chocolate cake** to keep the wolf at bay! Make sure you've got an adult to help you with this delicious recipe.*

YOU WILL NEED:

* 175g unsalted butter, softened
* 175g caster sugar
* 3 large eggs
* 150g self-raising flour
* 50g cocoa powder
* 1 teaspoon baking powder
* 1 teaspoon vanilla extract
* 20cm round cake tin, greased and lined with baking paper

1 Preheat the oven to 175°C (gas mark 4).

2 Mix the butter and sugar in a mixing bowl (make sure it's big enough for all the ingredients!).

3 Add the rest of the ingredients and beat together with an electric whisk or wooden spoon until the mixture is smooth.

4 Pour the mixture into your cake tin and pop it into the oven.

5 Bake for about 45 minutes, or until your cake looks golden and fully risen. Ask a grown-up to help you check the cake is full risen by sticking a skewer in the middle. If it comes out clean (with no cake mixture stuck to it) then the cake is ready to be taken out of the oven.

6 Enjoy!

IN THIS YEAR

1955
Fact Pack

What else was happening in the world when this Puffin book was published?

CATHERINE STORR

CLEVER POLLY AND THE STUPID WOLF

The first ever Guinness Book of Records is published.

Birds Eye cod fish fingers are introduced in Britain.

C. S. Lewis's book The Magician's Nephew – the sixth instalment in The Chronicles of Narnia – is published.

PUFFIN
WRITING
TIP

Listen to your favourite piece of music, then write about what you imagine as it plays.

If you have enjoyed *Clever Polly and the Stupid Wolf* you may like to read the next adventures of Polly and the very, very stupid wolf in *Polly and the Wolf Again* . . .

1. The Clever Wolf and Poor Stupid Little Polly (1)

THE WOLF sat at home in his kitchen, where he usually enjoyed himself so much; his elbows were on the table, and he was chewing, but there was no feeling of peace, of comfortable fullness, of not being likely to be hungry again for several hours, which was how the wolf liked to feel in his own house.

The table was covered with sheets of paper. Some of them had only a word or two written on them, some had a whole sentence. Most of them were blank.

Presently the wolf sighed, spat out the object he had been chewing – it was a pencil – and tried again. On a large, clean sheet of paper he wrote, laboriously:

'One day the Clever Wolf caught Polly and ate her all up!'

He stopped. He read what he had written. Then he read it again. He put the pencil back between his teeth and began to search among the sheets of paper for something. When he found it, he opened it flat on the table and leant over it, spelling out the longer words as he read. It was a book.

But reading did not seem much more satisfactory than writing. Every now and then the wolf snarled, and at last he shut the book up with a snap and pushed it away from him; but as he did so, his eyes fell on the cover, and the name of the book, printed there in large black letters:

CLEVER POLLY AND THE
STUPID WOLF

'It's so unfair!' he muttered angrily to himself. '*Clever* Polly, indeed! Just because she's managed to escape me for a time. And calling me stupid! Me! Why, I always used to win when we played Hide the Piglet as wolf cubs. "Stupid Wolf!" I'll show them. I'll write a book full of stories which will show how clever I am – far cleverer than that silly little Polly. I'll start the story of my life now, and then everyone will be able to see that it's not me that is stupid.'

He pulled another sheet of paper towards him.

'I was born,' he began writing in his untidy sprawling hand, 'in a large and comfortable hole, in the year –'

He stopped.

'Well, I know I'm about eleven,' he said to himself. 'So if I take eleven away from now, I shall know when I was born. Eleven away from … eleven away from … What am I taking eleven away from?'

'I'll do it with beans!' he thought, encouraging himself. 'It's always easier with beans.'

Leaving his pencil on the table, he got up and fetched a large canister of dried beans from a shelf over the stove. He shook a small shower out on the table; one or two fell on the floor.

'Nine, ten, eleven,' counted the wolf. He tipped the spare beans back into the canister.

'But I'm taking eleven away from something,' he remembered. He looked doubtfully into the tin and tipped it a little to see how full it was. The beans made an agreeable rattling sound as they slid about inside, and the wolf shook the canister gently several times to hear it again.

'There seem to be an awful lot of beans in there,' he said aloud. 'I wonder just what I've got to take eleven away from?'

He sat down to consider the point. Could it be eleven? He spread the eleven beans out on the table and looked at them. Then he took eleven beans off the table, counting them one by one.

'Eleven away leaves none. So eleven years ago was nothing. The year nothing. It seems a very long time ago.'

The wolf was puzzled. It did certainly seem a very long time ago, but it still didn't sound quite right. He could not remember ever having seen a book which gave as a date the year nothing.

'It can't be right,' he decided. 'It must be eleven away from something else. I wonder what it is? Who could I ask to tell me?'

There was, of course, only one answer to this, and five minutes later the wolf had walked down the path through the garden to Polly's front door and was ringing her bell.

'I'll talk to you from up here if you don't mind,' said Polly's voice from the first-floor window. 'Yes, Wolf, what can I do for you today?'

'You can tell me what I have to take eleven away from.'

'Eleven? Why eleven?'

'Because that is how old I am.'

'Why do you want to take how old you are away from anything?'

'Because I want to know what year it was.'

'What year what was?'

'The year I was born in, of course. Silly!' said the wolf triumphantly. 'I said it was Silly Polly and you are! What do I take it away from?'

'Nineteen fifty-seven.'

'And what do I have to do with it?' the wolf asked, now thoroughly muddled.

'You take that away from it.'

'What's That?'

'Eleven. Well, that's what you said,' Polly answered, a little confused herself.

'Don't go away,' pleaded the wolf. 'Let me get it straight in my head. I take eleven away from nineteen and then from fifty-seven and then –'

'No, stupid. Not from nineteen, from nineteen hundred and fifty-seven; and then the answer is the year you were born in!'

'Nineteen hundred!' said the wolf, appalled.

'And fifty-seven.'

'Nineteen hundred and fifty-seven. I don't think I've got enough beans,' said the wolf gloomily.

'I don't see how beans come into it,' Polly said. 'It's years you're counting in, not beans.'

'It's beans while I'm actually counting,' the wolf said firmly. 'And you're sure the answer is the year I was born?'

'Certain.'

'Thank you. Good morning,' the wolf called over his shoulder, as he trotted away down the garden path. He went home, sat down at his kitchen table and began to count out beans.

'A hundred and thirty-three, a hundred and thirty-four, a hundred and thirty-five ... Bother.'

The hundred and thirty-sixth bean was a very highly polished one. It slipped out of the wolf's paw, leapt nimbly into the air, fell on the floor, and rolled under the cooking stove.

'Bother, bother, BOTHER!' the wolf said out loud. He looked into the canister. There were only seven or eight beans left: he could not afford to lose one. He got down from his chair and lay flat on his front on the floor to look for the missing bean. It lay out of reach, right at the back of the cooker, against the wall, in company with a burnt chestnut and a very dirty toasting fork.

'My toasting fork!' the wolf exclaimed, delighted to see it again; it had been missing for several months. He retrieved the fork, dusted it with his tail, and used it to poke out the bean.

The wolf dusted the bean, said solemnly out loud, 'One hundred and thirty-six,' and put it on the table.

He gave a triumphant wave of his useful tail. Several beans were swept off the table and disappeared under various pieces of furniture.

'Oh —!' cried the wolf, enraged. He sat down at the table, staring angrily at the remaining beans. He tipped up the canister and added the rest of the beans to the pile he had already counted.

'A hundred and thirty-seven, a hundred and thirty-eight, a hundred and ... What's the use when I want nineteen hundred and something? I'll never be able to count the whole lot!'

He absent-mindedly put the last bean in his mouth. It wasn't too bad. He ate another.

'Easier with a spoon,' he murmured a minute or two later, and going to the dresser fetched a battered tablespoon. With its help he ate another two dozen beans fairly quickly.

'That's funny!' he thought after the second spoonful. 'I believe I generally eat these cooked. Very absent-minded I seem to be getting.'

He fetched a saucepan, filled it with water, and put it on the fire. When the water was boiling he tossed in the remaining beans, salt, pepper and herbs. He fried some rashers of bacon, an onion and a few mushrooms in a pan, and when everything was cooked he mixed it into a glorious mess together, added a tomato and, in a very few mouthfuls, swallowed the lot.

'Ah,' he said, wiping his mouth on the back of his paw, 'that's better. Now, let me see – What was I doing?'

He looked round the kitchen and his eye fell on the empty canister.

'Oh!' he said aloud. 'Bother!'

'Never mind,' he said. 'They tasted much better than they counted. Besides it would have taken me ages to get up to nineteen hundred and fifty-seven. I'd never have had time to write anything. After all what does it matter what year it was I was born? I'm here now, that's the important thing.'

He picked up the last sheet of paper he had written on and tore it across several times.

Then, sitting down, he pulled another towards him and wrote in a bolder hand:

THE CLEVER WOLF AND POOR STUPID POLLY

'Fortunately,' (the wolf wrote), 'I was born.'

Polly and the Wolf Again
is available in A Puffin Book.